EGMONT

We bring stories to life

This edition published in Great Britain 2011 by Dean,
an imprint of Egmont UK Limited
239 Kensington High Street, London W8 6SA
All rights reserved.

HiT entertainment

ISBN 978 0 6035 6620 2
1 3 5 7 9 10 8 6 4 2
Printed in China

Thomas and the Naughty Trick

Based on *The Railway Series* by The Rev. W. Awdry

One day, Thomas was fitted with a brand new whistle.

The whistle gleamed . . . and Thomas beamed!

He blew his new whistle all day long.

He blew it softly . . . and he blew it LOUDLY!

Thomas blew his new whistle in stations . . . and in Misty Valley.

Thomas thought it was the most wonderful whistle he'd ever had.

Thomas puffed into the Wharf, pulling a train of empty trucks behind him.

The Thin Controller was there to greet him.

"Thomas," said The Thin Controller, "the narrow gauge engines are bringing bricks, flour and timber."

He told Thomas that the bricks, flour and timber had to be loaded into his trucks by teatime.

Then The Thin Controller left.

Thomas was very happy to have such a special job and he blew his new whistle loudly.

Rheneas was so surprised that he JUMPED – and the pipes all fell off his trucks.

Thomas thought it was very funny!

"That was fun!" he tooted.

Thomas wanted to play more jokes on his friends.

Later that day, Rusty puffed into the Wharf, shunting trucks full of red bricks. The bricks were to be unloaded into Thomas' trucks.

Thomas rolled up behind Rusty.

The little engines held their puff as Thomas blew his new whistle. "PEEP!"

Rusty JUMPED – and biffed into his trucks. Suddenly, he was covered in red brick dust!

The little engines all laughed at poor Rusty.

Thomas thought it was tremendous fun!

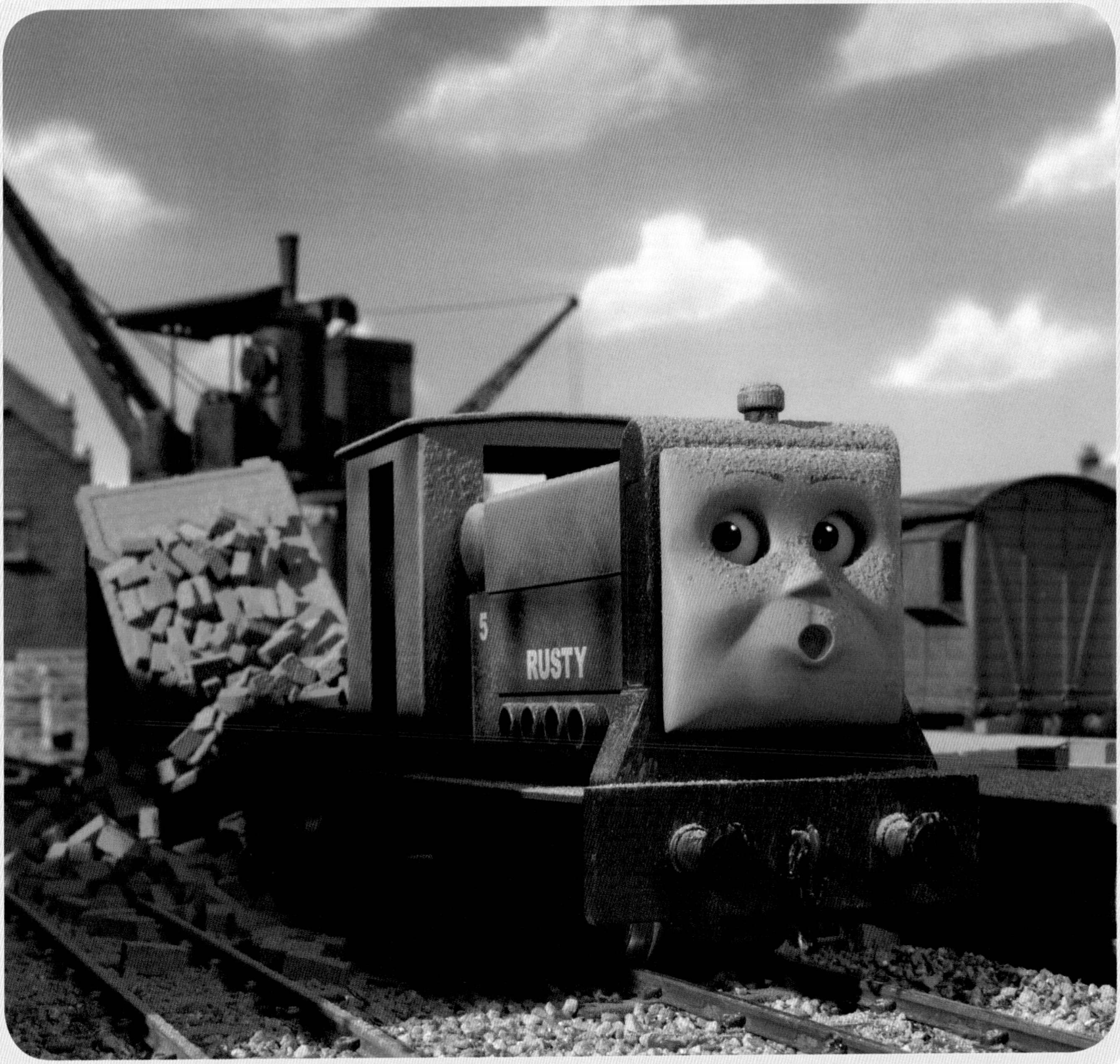
5
RUSTY

Rusty wanted to join in with all the fun the other engines were having.

"Can't catch me!" called Rusty, steaming around the Wharf.

Thomas puffed along beside him as everyone laughed.

They were all having so much fun . . . that they forgot about unloading the bricks!

Thomas had another idea.

"Sir Handel will be arriving with the trucks of flour soon," he tooted. "Why don't we all 'peep' him at once?"

The little engines thought it was a very exciting idea. They all found hiding places in the warehouse.

When Sir Handel puffed into the Wharf, there was nobody to be seen!

"Now!" Thomas cried, and he blew his new whistle as loudly as he could.

From their hiding places, the little engines blew their whistles, too!

"PEEP! PEEP!"

Sir Handel biffed his trucks in surprise – making flour fly up into the air like a great white cloud!

"You look like a ghost!" laughed Rusty.

Sir Handel thought it was very funny indeed.

"Woo!" he laughed. "Look at me – I'm a ghost!"

And he steamed away.

Soon, all the engines were chasing each other . . . and still no one was loading up Thomas' trucks with bricks!

Thomas had another idea.

"Peter Sam is on his way," tooted Thomas. "Let's 'peep' him as well!"

The little engines agreed this was a very good idea.

As Peter Sam trundled into the Wharf, Thomas got ready with his whistle . . .

The little engines got their whistles ready, too.

"PEEP!" went Thomas and the little engines.

Peter Sam shot forwards and bashed into his flatbeds, which were stacked with timber.

They burst through the buffers, smashed through a pile of oil drums . . .

. . . and SPLASHED straight into the canal!

"Oh my!" cried the little engines.

"Cinders and ashes!" gasped Thomas.

The Thin Controller arrived at the Wharf.

"What has been going on here?" he said, angrily. "There are bricks on the rails, there's flour all over the warehouse and timber in the canal!"

Thomas rolled forwards, looking guilty.

"I'm sorry, Sir," he wheeshed, sadly. "It's all my fault. I just wanted to play tricks and have some fun."

The Thin Controller was very cross.

"You must clear up this mess at once!" he cried. "And your trucks must be loaded by teatime."

Later on that day, The Thin Controller came back to check on the engines.

He saw Thomas looking pleased with himself. But he couldn't see Thomas' trucks!

"Where are your trucks?" asked The Thin Controller, very crossly.

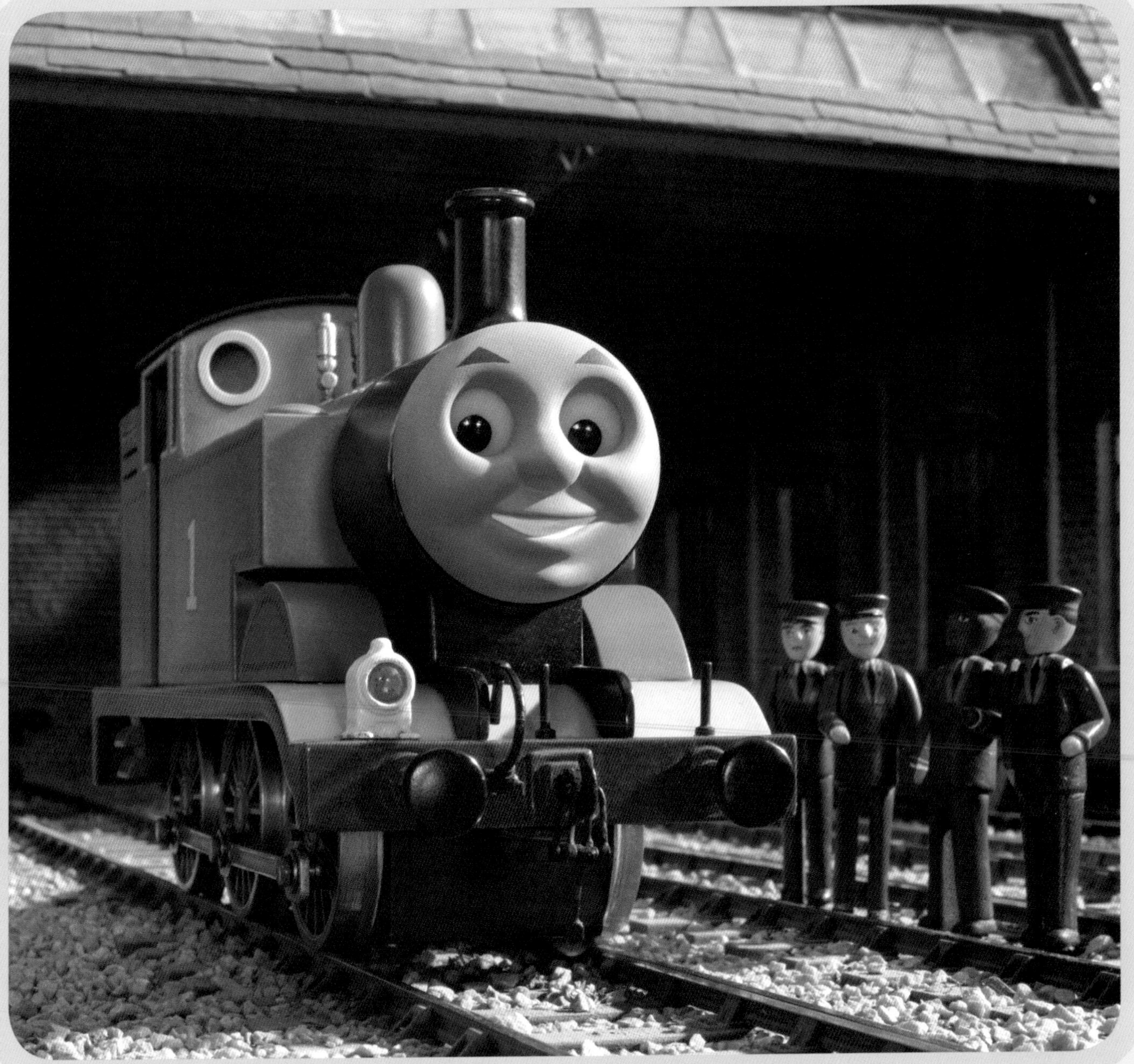

Thomas smiled to himself. He was playing another naughty trick!

He puffed forwards slowly so The Thin Controller could see the trucks, which were full of bricks, flour and timber. Thomas had been hiding them as a joke!

"Here they are, Sir!" he whistled, happily. "Loaded up and ready to go!"

The little engines laughed.

Soon, The Thin Controller was laughing, too. "That was a funny joke, Thomas!" he said. "You are a Really Funny Engine!"